YEARLING BOOKS

Since 1966, Yearling has been the

leading name in classic and award-winning

literature for young readers.

With a wide variety of titles,

Yearling paperbacks entertain, inspire,

and encourage a love of reading.

FAVORITES BY JUDY BLUME

Picture and Story Books
The Pain and the Great One
The One in the Middle Is the Green Kangaroo
Freckle Juice

The Pain and the Great One Chapter Books
Soupy Saturdays with the Pain and the Great One
Cool Zone with the Pain and the Great One
Going, Going, Gone! with the Pain and the Great One
Friend or Fiend? with the Pain and the Great One

The Fudge Books
Tales of a Fourth Grade Nothing
Otherwise Known as Sheila the Great
Superfudge
Fudge-a-Mania
Double Fudge

For Middle-Grade Readers
Iggie's House
Blubber
Starring Sally J. Freedman as Herself
It's Not the End of the World
Are You There God? It's Me, Margaret.
Then Again, Maybe I Won't
Deenie
Just as Long as We're Together
Here's to You, Rachel Robinson

For Young Adults
Tiger Eyes
Forever . . .
Letters to Judy: What Kids Wish They Could Tell You
*Places I Never Meant to Be: Original Stories by
Censored Writers* (edited by Judy Blume)

Judy Blume

Going, Going, Gone!

with the Pain & the Great One

ILLUSTRATIONS BY James Stevenson

A YEARLING BOOK

Text copyright © 2008 by P&G Trust
Illustrations copyright © 2008 by James Stevenson

All rights reserved. Published in the United States by Yearling, an imprint of Random House Children's Books, a division of Random House, Inc., New York. Originally published in hardcover in the United States by Delacorte Press, an imprint of Random House Children's Books, a division of Random House, Inc., New York, in 2008.

Yearling and the jumping horse design are registered trademarks of Random House, Inc.

Visit us on the Web! www.randomhouse.com/kids

Educators and librarians, for a variety of teaching tools, visit us at www.randomhouse.com/teachers

The Library of Congress has cataloged the hardcover edition of this work as follows:
Blume, Judy.
Going, going, gone! with the Pain and the Great One / Judy Blume ;
illustrations by James Stevenson.
p. cm.
Summary: Further adventures of first-grader Jake "the Pain" and his sister, third-grader Abigail "the Great One," include a trip to the beach with Grandma, to a county fair with Aunt Diana, and to a mall with Dad.
ISBN: 978-0-385-73307-6 (hardcover) — ISBN: 978-0-385-90326-4 (lib. bdg.)
[1. Brothers and sisters—Fiction. 2. Schools—Fiction. 3. Family life—Fiction.]
I. Stevenson, James, ill. II. Title.
PZ7.B6265 Goi 2008
[Fic]—dc22
2008006634

ISBN: 978-0-440-42094-1 (pbk.)

Printed in the United States of America

10 9

First Yearling Edition

With many thanks to my editor and publisher,
Beverly Horowitz,
who encouraged me to write down these stories
that have lived inside my head for so long.
It's been a treat working with you. Your support
and enthusiasm for this series and your friendship
over the years are so appreciated.

With love,
Judy

CONTENTS

The Pain

Meet
the
Pain

My sister's name is Abigail. I call her the Great One because she thinks she's so great. She says, "I don't think it, I know it!" When she says that I laugh like crazy. Then she gets mad. It's fun to make her mad. Who cares if she's in third grade and I'm just in first? That doesn't make her faster. Or stronger. Or even smarter. I don't get why Mom and Dad act like she's so special. Sometimes I think they love her more than me.

The Great One

Meet
the
Great One

My brother's name is Jacob but everyone calls him Jake. Everyone but me. I call him the Pain because that's what he is. He's a first-grade pain. And he will always be a pain—even if he lives to be a hundred. Even then, I'll be two years older than him. I'll still know more about everything. And I'll always know exactly what he's thinking. That's just the way it is. I don't get why Mom and Dad act like he's so special. Sometimes I think they love him more than me.

The Pain

THE LIZARD AND THE WOLF

Grandma rented a house at the beach. Yesterday we drove there. I got carsick. I almost always get carsick if the ride takes more than an hour. Under an hour, I'm okay. The Great One doesn't get it. She says, "That doesn't make any sense."

"It makes sense to me," I told her.

"A person either gets carsick or he

doesn't," she said. "Look at me—I don't get carsick, which makes me a good traveler."

"Does not!" I shouted.

"Does too!" she shouted back. "Mom, aren't I a good traveler?" Mom was driving. Dad was snoozing in the seat next to her.

"You're both good travelers," Mom said.

"But if you had to choose one of us to take on a trip, wouldn't you rather take the one who doesn't puke every time he gets in the car?" the Great One asked.

"No fair!" I called. "I don't puke *every* time."

"Children," Mom said. "I'm trying to concentrate on the road."

When we got to the beach, Grandma took us shopping while Mom and Dad unpacked. We're staying for a week. A week is a long time. Long enough to choose your favorite breakfast cereal. Mine is Cream of Wheat because it's white. I only like white foods. The Great One doesn't care what

color her food is. She chose Cheerios.

At the supermarket we followed Grandma down the Fun-in-the-Sun aisle. She tossed a tube of sunscreen into our cart. The Great One ran ahead to a display of Boogie boards. "I've always wanted a Boogie board," she told Grandma. "I could have so much fun in the ocean if only I had one." She looked through the stack of boards. "Oh, this one is so cool!" She held up a purple board. "Isn't this one cool, Grandma?" It had a picture of a lizard on it.

"You think it will be okay with your mom and dad?" Grandma asked.

"Oh, yes!" the Great One said. "I'm a good swimmer. You know what a good swimmer I am."

"Well, then—let's get it," Grandma said.

The Great One threw her arms around Grandma. "You're the best grandma in the history of the world!"

Grandma laughed. "Let's hope you think so the next time I say *no*." Then she looked at

me. "Would you like a Boogie board, Jake?"

"Don't waste your money," the Great One said. "He won't use it."

"Yes, I will!" I said. I chose a yellow board with a wolf's face on it.

The next day, before we headed for the beach, the Great One said, "I hope the waves are big today." Then she looked right at me and said, "I take that back. I hope they're huge!"

At the beach Dad set up the umbrella and opened the chairs. Grandma spread out the blanket while Mom reached into her bag for the new sunscreen. "You first, Abigail," she said to the Great One.

"Why do I have to get sunscreened first?" the Great One asked.

"I thought you *like* to go first," I said.

The Great One gave me one of her *looks*.

When Mom was done with us, the Great One grabbed her Boogie board and raced down to the ocean. Dad followed her. I followed Dad.

When I reached wet sand, I stopped. The waves weren't huge. But they weren't small, either. I watched as the Great One paddled out on her Boogie board. When she got far enough, she turned back and waved to Dad. Then she watched over her shoulder until just before the next wave started. When it did, she was on her board riding in to shore. Then she did it again. And again. She didn't care if her face got wet or if she fell off her board, or even if she went under a wave. Nothing stopped her.

When I got tired of watching, I started digging a hole. I dug deeper and deeper until the ocean came up inside it. Then I sat in the hole. The water was warm. Warmer than in the ocean.

The next day the Great One was at it again. She spent all afternoon in the ocean on her Boogie board, riding the waves to shore. She says it's the best fun she's ever had. She says I don't know what I'm missing.

"You *have* to try it, Jake!" she said the next morning while I was eating my Cream of Wheat.

"Try what?" I asked, like I didn't know.

"Your Boogie board!"

"I'm waiting," I told her.

"Waiting for what?" she asked.

"The perfect wave."

"Ha!" she said, laughing.

That afternoon I decided to build a sand fort. Grandma helped me. "I have a lot of experience," she said. "I used to help your mom build sand castles when she was your age."

"With moats around them?" I asked.

"Oh, sure," Grandma said. "They all had moats."

Grandma was good at making turrets and drizzling wet sand on top of them. But after a while she fanned her face with her hat and said, "Whew—it's hot out today. Time for a swim. Want to come in with me, Jake?"

"Not now," I told her. "I have to stay here and guard my fort." I watched as Grandma dove under a wave.

Sometimes I go into the ocean up to my knees. But no higher—not even when I'm with Dad. Because higher means the waves could crash over your head. No way will I ever dive under a wave. Not if I live to be a hundred million years old!

When Mom called us for snacks, the Great One said, "You're the only kid on the beach who won't go into the ocean."

"Am not!" I told her.

"Are too!" the Great One said. She was peeling a tangerine. "Do you want everyone to think you're afraid? Do you want everyone to think you're a baby?" She shoved a piece of tangerine into her mouth.

"I'm not a baby!" I shouted, grabbing a juice box. "I know how to swim in a pool."

"You call the doggie paddle swimming?"

"Yes!"

"Then why don't you pretend the ocean is a big pool?"

"I don't like salt water in my eyes," I told her. "And I don't want it up my nose, either!"

"Wear a mask," the Great One called as she ran back toward the ocean with her lizard Boogie board.

That night on the boardwalk I saw a store window filled with masks. I asked Grandma if we could go inside. She took my hand and we went into the store together.

I checked out all the masks. I tried on Spider-Man first. Next I tried on Batman. Then I tried on a mask that looked like the President. After that, one that looked like a gorilla.

When Grandma walked away to look at something else, I saw it. The perfect mask— the *Wolfman*! I pulled it on and crept up behind Grandma. Then I poked her in the ribs and growled. Grandma jumped a foot off the floor and shrieked so loud she scared me. Everyone in the store turned to look at us. At least, I think they did. It wasn't that easy to see what was going on from inside the Wolfman mask.

When Grandma calmed down, she laughed. "You surprised me, Jake!"

"I could tell," I said.

"Would you like that mask?"

I wasn't going to ask for it, but if Grandma wanted to buy it for me, it wouldn't be nice to say no. So I said, "Sure. Thanks a lot, Grandma!"

"You're welcome, *precious*."

Precious is what Grandma calls me when no one else is around. It's our secret word.

I pulled off the Wolfman mask and plunked it on the counter.

"Getting an early start on Halloween?" the cashier said.

"No," I told him. But I don't think he believed me.

The next day at the beach, after the Great One raced into the ocean, I pulled on my Wolfman mask. Dad said, "That's a scary mask, Jake. I hope you don't scare your sister."

I was hoping I would.

I grabbed my yellow Boogie board with the wolf face on it and carried it down to the ocean's edge. Then I stood on the board, like I was a surfer.

"Look, Mommy," I heard a little kid say. "That boy thinks it's Halloween."

Was he talking about me?

It was hot inside my Wolfman mask. Hot and sweaty. Soon I felt like pulling it off and dumping a bucket of water over my head. Water from the sink, not ocean water.

When the Great One came out of the ocean, she said, "Why are you wearing that thing? You look like a dork!"

"I look like the Wolfman," I told her.

"You think the Wolfman wears a bathing suit?"

"He does when he goes to the beach," I said.

"The Wolfman is covered with hair," she said, "in case you didn't know."

"He shaves it off in summer."

She laughed.

17

So I shouted, "You *said* to wear a mask, remember?"

"I meant a *dive* mask," she said, "not a Halloween mask!"

"That's how much you know!" I told her. "Because this is a—" I had to think fast. "This is a *surfer* mask."

"A *surfer* mask?" The Great One laughed again.

"If you don't believe me, just ask the man at the store!"

She was quiet for a minute. "He really told you it was a *surfer* mask?" she said. I knew she was looking at me. I could see her legs but not her face.

"Yes, all the real surfers have them." I was so hot I didn't think I could last another minute inside my Wolfman mask.

"Let me try it," the Great One said.

I pulled off my mask and handed it to her. It felt so good to be out of it.

I dumped a bucket of *ocean* water over my head. I was careful to keep my eyes shut.

"How do I look?" the Great One asked. She was posing like a surfer in my Wolfman mask. She looked totally stupid. But I said, "You look cool."

Then she was off, racing out to catch the next wave. But she missed and fell off her board. She fell off on her next try too. And the one after that.

She whipped off the Wolfman mask and came tearing out of the ocean. "This mask doesn't work!" she shouted, waving it in the

air. "You tricked me, you little pain! You won't get away with this!"

But I was already racing down the beach, hoping she would never catch me.

The Great One

EXTRAVAGANZA

Part One

Aunt Diana took us to the county fair. She bought each of us twenty tickets. "I can't believe how much these tickets cost," she said. "Use them carefully."

"We will," I told her.

"I'm going on the Gravitron," the Pain told me as Aunt Diana walked ahead of us, pushing the baby in his stroller.

"No, you're not," I said. "You have to be at least twelve to go on the Gravitron."

"Ha ha," he sang. "That's how much you know!"

I know plenty about the Gravitron. I know I'm never going on it. It spins around so fast it pins you against the wall while the floor disappears from under you. I learned about it from a TV show called *Amusement Ride Extravaganzas*.

Aunt Diana turned to us and said, "Let's see the farm animals first. Before the baby falls asleep."

The Pain leaned over and whispered to me, "Then the Gravitron!"

The farm animals were in a big barn. First came the pigs. The baby clapped his hands and said "Uh-oh!" Then came the goats and fancy chickens and rabbits. The baby said "Uh-oh!" to everything.

When we came out of the barn, the Pain poked me. "Time for the Gravitron!"

But Aunt Diana had other ideas. "Let's do the food hall next."

"Is the food hall like the food court at the mall?" the Pain asked.

Aunt Diana laughed. "Not exactly," she said.

The food hall was filled with homegrown vegetables. The Pain kept running ahead, announcing what was coming next.

"An eggplant that's bigger than the baby!"

"A tomato so huge it could be somebody's head!"

The baby clapped his hands and said, "Uh-oh!"

When we came out of the food hall, Aunt Diana sat on a bench under a tree and gave the baby a bottle. The way things were going, I thought we'd never get to the rides. So I said, "Oh, look, Aunt Diana, there's the Super Slide! The Super Slide is my favorite."

"Mine is the Gravitron," the Pain said, jumping up and down.

"Gravitron?" Aunt Diana said. "What's that?"

"It's where you spin around so fast you're mashed against the wall," the Pain said. "It's an *extravaganza*!"

"Whoa . . . that's a big word," Aunt Diana said.

"He learned it from a TV show called *Amusement Ride Extravaganzas*," I explained. "You have to be at least twelve to go on it."

"Unless you're with a grown-up," the Pain told Aunt Diana. "And you'll take me, won't you?"

"I'm sorry, Jake," Aunt Diana said, "but rides give me vertigo."

"Is that like vomit?" the Pain asked.

"Vertigo is dizziness," Aunt Diana said. "Rides make me dizzy, and that doesn't feel good."

"The Gravitron won't make you dizzy," the Pain said. "It only lasts eighty seconds."

"The longer you stand here blabbing, the longer it's going to take on line at the Super Slide," I said, tapping my foot.

"Okay," Aunt Diana said. "Here's the deal. You two can get on line at the Super Slide. I'll keep an eye on you from here. Then, as soon as I've fed the baby, I'll meet you. Okay?"

"Okay." I grabbed the Pain's hand and pulled him with me. But on the way to the

Super Slide he spotted the cotton candy stand.

"I want blue," he said.

"After the Super Slide," I told him.

"No, now!" And he used up five of his tickets buying himself a blue cotton candy. I don't like cotton candy. It feels like fuzz in my mouth.

The guy in charge of the Super Slide had a tattoo on his arm. We each handed him four tickets and got on line. I took a swig from my water bottle. It was hot in the sun and the line for the Super Slide wrapped around twice.

"Cotton candy makes me thirsty," the Pain said, watching me drink. "I need water."

"Where's your water bottle?" I asked.

"I left it in the car. Can I share with you?"

"Share my water bottle?" I said. "Ewww, no, thank you."

"But I'm thirsty," the Pain said. "I might die of thirst. Then you'll be sorry."

I didn't answer.

"Okay, fine," he said. "I'll go buy a water bottle."

"That's going to cost a lot of tickets," I said. But did he listen? Does he ever listen?

The Pain came back with a water bottle and a toy mouse. "For Fluzzy," he said, walking the mouse up my arm.

"How much did you pay for that?"

"Three tickets for the mouse, and five for the water." He chugged down half the water at once. The line for the Super Slide moved so slowly I thought we'd never get to the stairs leading to the top. I checked my watch. Five minutes went by, then ten minutes, then fifteen. The Pain finished his water.

Finally, we made it to the stairs. Just as we started to go up, the Pain grabbed my arm. "I have to pee."

"Now?" I asked.

He nodded.

"But it's almost our turn," I told him. "Can't you wait until we're done?"

He shook his head. "You have to come with me so I don't get lost."

"But we'll lose our place on line." I could

30

see he didn't care. I could see it was getting to be an emergency.

I turned to the girls behind us, who were older than me. "I have to take my brother to the bathroom. Will you hold our place?"

They looked at the Pain. He was shifting his weight from leg to leg. Then they looked at each other. One of them smiled and said, "Sure, we'll hold your place for three tickets."

"Three tickets?"

"That's three tickets *each*," the other one said. "Because there are two of you."

Then the first one said, "That's six tickets, in case you can't add."

"Hurry!" the Pain said to me.

"Give me three tickets," I told him.

He handed them over. I shoved the six tickets at the girls.

We raced to the Porta Potties. Another long line. "I can't wait!" the Pain cried.

So I went up to the guy who was next. "We have an emergency situation," I told him.

He looked at the Pain, who was holding the front of his pants. "I've been in a few emergency situations myself," he said. And he let the Pain go next.

When he came out, we ran back to the Super Slide. But when we tried to get through the gate, Mr. Tattoo said, "Where do you think you're going?"

"Back to our place," I told him.

He shook his head. "Four tickets each, then end of the line, same as everyone else."

"But we already paid! And we stood on line for twenty minutes!" I told him. "If you don't believe me you can ask those girls at the top of the stairs. We were right in front of them." I called to the girls, "Hey . . ." But they were already sliding down.

"Hey!" I called again when they got to the bottom.

They pretended not to hear me.

"We paid them six tickets to hold our place!" I told Mr. Tattoo.

He laughed. "You expect me to believe that?" he said. "Don't you know what happens to children who lie?"

"I'm not lying! And if you don't let us back in, I'm telling my aunt." I grabbed the Pain's hand. "Come on," I said. "We're going to get Aunt Diana."

As soon as we turned away, Mr. Tattoo called, "Okay . . . okay . . ." Then he opened the gate and let us cut the line. "But no more funny business!"

I didn't answer because we were already climbing the stairs as fast as we could. When we got to the top, I looked down. We were so high! I was afraid I'd get *vomitigo* like Aunt Diana. We spread out our rugs, sat on them, and on the count of three, we let go. Whoosh! We slid faster and faster, until it felt like we were flying! Flying over the bumps with the wind blowing our hair and the speed taking our breath away. I heard myself scream. I heard the Pain laugh. And then, just like that, it was over. We were at the bottom.

"Want to go again?" I asked the Pain.

But the Pain had other ideas. And I couldn't get him to change his mind.

Part Two

The Gravitron was off by itself. It looked like a spaceship with flashing lights. The Pain ran ahead of me. When I caught up to him, he was in front of the sign that read

SIX TICKETS PER RIDE
NO ONE UNDER 12 ALLOWED
UNLESS ACCOMPANIED
BY AN ADULT

The Pain searched for his tickets. He turned his pockets inside out. Finally he cried, "I have no more tickets!"

I could have told him that. If he hadn't wasted his tickets on blue cotton candy, a water bottle, and that mouse, he'd still have thirteen tickets left, like me. "Here," I said, handing him six tickets. "Have a good time. I'll wait for you."

He couldn't believe I forked over six tickets just like that. But I knew my tickets were safe. I knew they weren't going to let him go by himself.

The Pain took the six tickets up to the woman in charge. She had spiky purple hair. "What's this?" she asked.

"It's six tickets to ride the Gravitron," he said.

She tapped the sign. "No one under twelve without an adult."

"I'm not under twelve," the Pain told her. "I'm just small for my age."

Purple Hair laughed. "Come back in ten years," she said.

"Everyone in my family is small," the Pain argued. He pointed at me. "Look at my aunt Abigail. . . ."

Oh, great! I thought. *Now I'm supposed to be his aunt.*

Purple Hair looked over at me. "I'm supposed to believe *she's* your aunt?" The Pain stood behind her making signs at me. So I stood as straight and tall as I could and gave her the *evil eye*. I don't know what the *evil eye* is exactly, but I once read about it in a scary book.

"I told you we were all small," the Pain said. "And it's not nice of you to make fun of small people."

While the Pain and Purple Hair were arguing, a long line of teenagers were handing her tickets and piling into the Gravitron.

Then I heard Aunt Diana calling, "Abigail, Jake! What are you doing here? You were supposed to wait for me."

"We are waiting. We're waiting here at the Gravitron!" the Pain told her.

Purple Hair checked out Aunt Diana. "Are you the mother?"

"I'm his aunt," Aunt Diana said.

"My *other* aunt," the Pain said.

Aunt Diana looked confused. But before the Pain could explain, a big guy came by with a couple of teenage boys. "Diana!" he called.

Aunt Diana looked up. "Rick!" she sounded surprised. She whispered to us, "It's my boss!"

37

"What are you doing here?" Rick asked.

"I'm with my niece and nephew," Aunt Diana told him. "What about you?"

"I'm with my son and his friends."

In less than two seconds the Pain made his move. He tugged on Rick's arm. "Will you take me on the Gravitron? It only takes eighty seconds. I'll give you all my tickets if you do."

I didn't remind him that he had no more tickets. Or that he owed me six.

"Jake," Aunt Diana said. "It's not polite to ask—"

But Rick stopped her before she finished. "No, it's okay. Maybe this will prove to my son I've still got what it takes." He handed Purple Hair the tickets. Then he took the Pain's hand, and they disappeared into the Gravitron.

"Uh-oh!" the baby said.

I was thinking the same thing.

The Gravitron started turning, slowly at first, then faster and faster, until it was whirling. The flashing lights blurred into a hundred colors. The music played louder and louder.

I wondered what it was like inside. I wondered why I was scared to try it but the Pain wasn't. He's afraid of the ocean and I'm not. He still sleeps with his stuffed elephant. He gets carsick! He's probably going to get sick from the Gravitron, too. They'll probably have to carry him out.

Eighty seconds later the Gravitron slowed down. Then it came to a stop. The teenagers piled out. Some of them were laughing like crazy. Some of them lined up to go again. One girl was crying. The Pain was smiling. But not Rick.

Rick's face was pale. He was holding his chest. "Rick!" Aunt Diana cried. "Are you all right?"

Rick sat down on a bench. "Just give me a minute." He took some deep breaths. Aunt Diana handed him her water bottle. He took a long drink. "Do you know what it's like in there?"

"I've no idea," Aunt Diana said.

"Believe me," Rick said. "You don't want to know."

I pulled the Pain aside. "What was it like?"

"It was an *extravaganza*!" He jumped up and down.

"And you didn't get sick?" I asked.

"Why would I get sick?"

Then Aunt Diana called, "Jake, come over here."

I followed him over to Aunt Diana. The baby clapped when he saw us.

Aunt Diana said, "Jake . . . don't you have something to say to Rick?"

At first the Pain didn't know what he was supposed to say. I could tell by the look on his face. Then he started smiling and dancing all around. "Hey, Rick . . ." he called. "Want to go again?"

The Pain

THE FURRY BOOGER

We have a pussy willow tree behind our house. Justin and Dylan came over after school today and the three of us picked pussy willows. We took off our shoes and socks and stuck pussy willows between our toes. They felt soft and tickly. We tried walking around without losing them. Then Dylan picked another pussy willow. "Watch this!" he said, and this time he stuck it up his nose.

Justin said, "Don't do that!"

"Why not?" Dylan asked. "I can blow it out any time I want." He held his other nostril shut and blew until the pussy willow came flying out.

That made us laugh.

"See? I told you," he said. He picked another pussy willow and stuck it up his other nostril.

So I picked a pussy willow and stuck it up my nose.

"Come on, Justin . . ." Dylan said.

"Oh . . . okay," Justin said. And he did it too.

We decided to have a contest to see who could blow their pussy willow the farthest. We made a line with a couple of sticks and stood behind it. Then all three of us blew at once. Dylan's pussy willow flew out and landed on the other side of our line. Justin's came out, but it just dropped to the ground and lay there next to his foot. I blew and blew but nothing happened.

"Try again," Dylan said.

So I did. Still nothing.

"Let me look," Justin said. He looked up my nose, then shook his head. "I don't see anything. Are you *sure* it didn't come out?"

"I can feel it," I said. "It's like having a big furry booger up my nose."

Dylan and Justin laughed. But I didn't. Justin said, "Get your magnifying glass, Jake."

"Can't," I told him. "I gave it to my sister."

"Go ask your sister if we can borrow it," Justin said.

"You come with me."

So the three of us went inside and up to the Great One's room. Fluzzy was curled up on her bed. He sat up when he heard us. The Great One was at her desk, cutting pictures out of a magazine.

"We need to borrow the magnifying glass," I told her.

"What for?" she said.

"We have to study something." I looked at Justin and Dylan. They nodded.

"What?" she asked. "What do you have to study?"

"We need to study a pussy willow," I told her.

She slid open her desk drawer and took out the magnifying glass. "Give it to me."

That made Dylan and Justin laugh.

The Great One looked over at them. "What's so funny?"

Dylan covered his mouth and Justin looked up at the ceiling.

"I don't have all day," she said. "I'm a very busy person. So either hand over the pussy willow or go away."

"It's in a . . . in a . . ." I started to say.

"In a *what*?" She looked at me. Now she was really interested.

"It's in a private place," I whispered.

"I'm not letting this magnifying glass out of my sight," the Great One said. "If you

48

want to use it, you have to show me the pussy willow."

Before I could say anything, Dylan blurted it out. "He can't show you. It's up his nose!"

"Your nose?" the Great One said, looking at me. "Ewww . . . that's the most disgusting thing I ever heard! What's it doing in there?"

"It's stuck!" Justin called.

"You have a pussy willow stuck up your nose?" she asked me.

When I didn't answer, she dashed into the hall calling, "Charlie . . . Charlie . . . come quick!"

Charlie is our babysitter. She's on the track team at her college. In two seconds she was up the stairs, sweeping everything out of her way, including Justin and Dylan. "What's the problem?"

"The Pain has a pussy willow stuck up his nose!" the Great One told her.

"What?" Charlie said, like she must have heard wrong.

"A pussy willow . . . stuck up his

nose!" the Great One repeated.

"Can you blow it out?" Charlie asked me.

"He tried," Justin and Dylan said together.

"I tried," I told Charlie.

Charlie flew back down the stairs. The rest of us followed. Fluzzy took a flying leap off the bed. Maybe he thought we were playing a game and he didn't want to miss the fun. Only *I* knew it wasn't going to be any fun. Not for me.

In the kitchen Charlie whipped out Mom's emergency book, the one with all the numbers and lists. She called Dr. Bender's office and told them I had a pussy willow stuck up my nose. Then she listened. When she hung up, she said, "Dr. Bender's not in the office today. His nurse said we should go straight to the ER."

"That means emergency room!" Justin sang. He sounded excited. Like we were going to a magic show.

"I went to the emergency room once,"

Dylan said. "When I broke my foot." He sounded like he was going to the same show.

"And that's where I got my stitches!" The Great One pulled up one leg of her jeans and showed us her scar. "Fourteen of them," she said proudly, like it was the most fun she ever had.

"I don't want to go to the emergency room!" I told them.

"You should have thought of that before you shoved a pussy willow up your nose," the Great One said.

"I need Mom," I told Charlie.

"I'm calling her cell right now," Charlie said.

But Mom didn't pick up, so Charlie left a message.

"I need Bruno," I said, heading upstairs.

At the ER we waited. We waited and waited and waited. Babies cried. People coughed. Somebody moaned. The Great One played Go Fish with Justin and Dylan. I leaned against Charlie and said, "Where's Mom?"

"She's on her way."

"When will she be here?"

"Before it's your turn."

But then it *was* my turn and Mom still wasn't there.

They put me on a table with wheels and pulled white curtains all around. Charlie

came inside the curtains. The Great One followed her. Justin and Dylan stood outside, peeking in.

The doctor wore blue scrubs with a white coat over them. She had a stethoscope around her neck. "I'm Dr. Itchee," she said.

"That's a funny name," I said.

She stuck a thermometer in my ear.

"I don't have a fever," I told her.

"It's routine," she said. Next she grabbed one of those doctor sticks. "Open your mouth and say 'aaah.'"

"I don't have a sore throat," I told her.

"It's routine," she said. Then she put the ends of her stethoscope in her ears. "Now let's have a listen."

I started to say, "And I don't have a . . ." but she said, "Shhh. . . ."

After that she wanted to feel my belly. I felt like shouting, *The pussy willow is up my nose!* But I didn't. Instead, I told Charlie, "I want my mom."

"I know it, sweetie." Charlie petted my head like I was Fluzzy. She doesn't have permission to call me *sweetie*. Only Mom is allowed to call me that. But I was glad she was there, so I didn't say anything. I didn't even tell the Great One to take her hand off my arm.

Next Dr. Itchee said, "Can you lie back and hold very, very still?"

"Maybe," I said.

Dr. Itchee pulled on doctor gloves. I held Bruno against me. I was scared but not *that* scared. First Dr. Itchee looked up my nose with a light. *"Aha!"* she said. She sounded like the magician who came to Dylan's birthday party. He was always saying "Aha!"

"It's really up there," Dr. Itchee said. She put her light away. "Okay, Jake . . . I'm going in now." It sounded like she was going to shrink herself into a teeny, tiny doctor and crawl up my nostril.

But then I saw the long, pointy tweezers heading for my nose and I shoved them out of the way. "No!" I yelled.

Dr. Itchee said, "I can't do this unless you keep still."

"He's scared," the Great One said.

"I think this might be easier if you both waited outside," Dr. Itchee said to Charlie and the Great One.

"But I *need* them!" I told Dr. Itchee. "They have to stay."

"All right," Dr. Itchee said. "But your sister has to be quiet. Can you be quiet?" she asked the Great One.

I would have laughed except I was too scared. For once, the Great One didn't say anything. She just nodded.

"This won't hurt if you hold still," Dr. Itchee told me. "And it will only take a minute. That's sixty seconds. Can you count to sixty?"

"Of course he can count to sixty!" the Great One said. "He's in first grade."

Dr. Itchee shot the Great One a look. The Great One covered her mouth and said, "Oops!"

I held on to Bruno and squeezed my eyes shut.

Then Dr. Itchee said, "You can start counting now. Don't forget to say 'one hundred' between each number."

The Great One counted with me.

"One–one hundred, two–one hundred, three–one hundred." I felt something cold inside my nose. I held Bruno tighter. "Four–one hundred, five–one hundred, six–one hundred . . ."

Then I felt the cold thing come out of my nose and Dr. Itchee said, "Got it!"

That's when Mom came rushing in with Dylan and Justin right behind her. Mom gave me a big hug. "Sweetie," she said. "You're so brave!" She kissed me and kept patting my head.

"He's not *that* brave," the Great One said.

Justin and Dylan gave me high fives. Then Dr. Itchee sat on the edge of my table.

"Okay, boys," she said. "I want you to listen carefully to what I'm going to say." She looked from Dylan to Justin to me. "Are you listening?" she asked.

We all nodded.

"Never, and I mean *never*, put anything up your nose that doesn't belong there."

"What belongs there?" Justin asked.

"Maybe nose spray," Dr. Itchee said. "But only if the doctor prescribes it. And never put anything in your ears, either. Not even a Q-tip."

"How about between your toes?" Dylan said.

"Between your toes is okay," Dr. Itchee said. "There's no place for it to get lost. But never put anything in any of your bodily orifices."

"Body *offices?*" I started thinking about having offices inside my body. And every day tiny people would go to work there.

"Orifices," Dr. Itchee said.

"They don't know that word," Mom told her.

"Even *I* don't know that word," the Great One said. "And I know a lot of words."

"It means openings," Dr. Itchee said. "And in this case it means bodily openings."

"You mean holes?" Justin asked.

"Yes," Dr. Itchee said. "Nothing goes in any of your—"

"Holes!" Dylan sang. Then the three of us laughed.

Dr. Itchee sighed. "Let's call them bodily openings, okay?"

"What about food?" Justin asked. "Food goes into your mouth and that's a—"

"Hole!" Dylan sang again.

Mom said, "Boys—listen to Dr. Itchee. She's trying to tell you something important."

"Thank you," Dr. Itchee said to Mom. "Jake was lucky today. But I've seen kids who weren't so lucky. So I want you all to promise you'll never do that."

"I promise," I said.

"Me too," Dylan said, "even though it was a fun game!"

Justin said, "I already knew not to put anything up my nose because my dad's a doctor."

Dr. Itchee looked surprised. "Then why did you do it?"

Justin shrugged. "Because my friends did."

"Just because your friends do something doesn't mean you should."

Justin's face turned red. He looked like he was going to cry. Mom said, "I think Justin knows that now. I think they all understand. Right, boys?"

We nodded. Then I said, "Can we go home now?"

Dr. Itchee said we could.

"And can I take that furry booger with me?" I asked.

"Euwww . . ." the Great One said. "That would be so disgusting!"

"I like being disgusting," I told her.

"And you're really good at it!" she said.

"Thanks," I answered.

"You're not welcome."

I laughed with my friends. Then we all went out for ice cream.

The Great One

KAPOOIE ONE

Yesterday it snowed. The first snow of the season. We built a snowman and put Dad's old rain hat on top of his head. But last night it rained and made a mess of the snow. It's still raining. A rainy December Sunday. Not that Dad's rain hat is helping our snowman. I watched out the window as he melted away.

When he was just about gone, Dad

called, "Who wants to go to a movie at the mall?"

"I do," the Pain shouted. "I want to see *Fried*."

"No fair!" I said. Because who wants to see a stupid movie about a bunch of robots trying to fry each other? "I want to see *Unicorn*."

"*Unicorn?*" the Pain said. "That's a *girl* movie!"

"Is not!" I told him. "It's about two boys and a girl."

"But it's still a *girl* movie!"

"We'll only go if you can compromise," Dad told us.

"What's compo . . . what's that word?" the Pain asked.

"Compromise," Dad said. "It means decide together. It means if Abigail wants red and Jake wants blue . . ."

Before Dad could finish I called, "We choose purple!"

"Good thinking, Abigail," Dad said.

I smiled. I like being a good thinker.

Then Dad added, "But that's not necessarily the way it works, because maybe there is no purple. Maybe you have to decide on either red or blue because those are the only choices."

"I know," I said to Dad. "You can take the Pain to see *Fried* and Mom can take me to see *Unicorn*." I knew *that* was good thinking!

But Dad said, "Mom needs the afternoon off to catch up on work."

"Okay," the Pain said, just like that. "I'll see the unicorn movie."

"You will?" I asked.

"Yes," he said. "Because I'm a good compo . . ."

"Compromiser," Dad said.

That made me mad. "How come you didn't give me the chance to prove what a good compromiser I am?" I asked Dad.

"I'm sure you'll have the chance to prove how well you can compromise very soon." Dad checked his watch. "Go and get ready. We'll have lunch at the food court."

"Yay, the food court!" the Pain shouted. "I want pizza!"

"I want burritos!" I shouted louder.

"Pizza!"

"Burritos!"

64

"Children," Dad said. "It's time for another compromise."

"So soon?" I asked.

"I told you you'd get the chance to prove how well you can compromise," Dad said to me.

But before I could say anything, the Pain sang, "Okay, I'll have burritos."

"Yay . . . burritos!" I sang.

"Not so fast, Abigail," Dad said. "You got to choose the movie. Jake gets to choose which kind of food to have."

"But Dad . . . he only eats white food. Doesn't that make it unfair?"

"There's no restaurant in the food court that serves only white food," Dad reminded me. "So I don't think you have to worry about that."

The Pain was smiling that sly smile of his.

"Okay," I said. "Pizza."

The Pain shouted, "Yay . . . pizza!"

The mall was crowded. Holiday music was

playing and there were decorations everywhere. A big cardboard Santa held a sign pointing to Santa's Workshop. That reminded me of something. So I started telling Dad this story about when I was little and Aunt Diana took me to Macy's to see Santa and I cried because when I sat on Santa's lap he kept *ho-ho-ho*-ing in my face and he had the most disgusting breath ever.

Dad said, "Was Jake there too?"

"Jake isn't in this story," I said.

"Who wants to be in your boring old story?" the Pain mumbled.

My story got longer and longer because one thing led to another and Dad finally said, "How does this story end, Abigail?"

And I said, "It ends . . . it ends when . . . um . . ." And then I looked over at the Pain but he wasn't there. I turned and checked behind me. He wasn't there either. I looked all around. But he wasn't anywhere. So I tugged Dad's arm and said, "Where's the Pain?"

"I thought you said Jake isn't in this story."

"Dad—I mean he's gone. One minute he was next to me and then *kapooie*—just like that, he wasn't."

Dad looked in every direction. Then he ran up and down the mall, calling "Jake . . . Jake . . . where are you?"

I tried to catch up with him. "Dad . . . wait!"

By then Dad had found a security guard. "My son!" Dad said. He sounded out of breath. "My son is missing!"

The security guard went into action, pressing numbers on his walkie-talkie. "Don't worry, sir," he said to Dad. "We deal with this all the time."

"His name is Jake," Dad told the security guard. "He's six years old."

"He'll be seven in April," I added.

"He's missing his top two front teeth," Dad said. "He has brown hair and brown eyes, and he's wearing a . . . a . . ."

I finished for him. "A gray sweatshirt with a big kangaroo on the front. Aunt Diana brought it back from Australia, and . . ."

Before I could finish telling about the Pain's clothes we were at the security station. Mom's told us a million times, if we ever get separated at the mall, we should tell a security guard. She says he'll take us to the

68

security station and that's where she'll come to find us. Maybe the Pain forgot our plan, because he wasn't there. And no one had heard anything about a boy who was lost.

Suddenly, I heard a man's voice over the loudspeaker. "Attention, shoppers! We have a missing six-year-old boy last seen near Toy City. If you see him, notify security immediately." Then he described the Pain. After that he said, "Stay where you are, Jake. We're going to find you."

"Try to stay calm, sir," another security guard said to Dad.

I wanted to tell him my dad is always calm. I wanted to say there's no one in the whole world who's more calm than my dad! But I didn't. Because I could see in Dad's eyes that he was worried. And seeing Dad that way was scary. If I was the one who was lost, Dad wouldn't be worried. He'd just say, *Abigail, we missed our movie because of you.*

Now there were security guards everywhere, and regular police too. I could see them from the window of the security station. Some of them were driving around in carts. And the loudspeakers didn't let up.

"We'll find him," the guard told Dad.

"I know we will," Dad said. "We have to."

And then you can tell him what a pain he is! I thought. *And how he made us miss our movie!* I didn't actually say any of that out loud. Because I started to think of the Pain being lost and scared. Then I got scared and grabbed Dad.

"It's going to be okay, Abigail," he said.

"Promise?" I asked.

He hugged me. "Promise."

The Pain

KAPOOIE TWO

The Great One's story was so boring I stopped listening. When we passed Toy City, I saw a big crowd. I wondered what all those kids were looking at. I wiggled my way up front to see. And there it was— a giant robot made of LEGOs, walking up and down in the window. I pressed my face against the glass. That robot was way bigger than Dad. That robot was huge! It was incredible. It was the most incredible LEGO toy ever! "Can you believe it?" I said to the Great One. "Don't you wish someone would give you *that* for Christmas or Hanukkah?" We're lucky because we have a Christmas grandpa and a Hanukkah grandma.

The Great One said, "Yes, I would like that LEGO set. How about you? What else do you wish you could have?"

I looked up then, because that voice didn't sound anything like the Great One. And when I did I got a big surprise—because it *wasn't* the Great One! It was some other girl. She was maybe in fifth grade. "You're not my sister!" I shouted.

And she answered, "Did I say I was?"

"No, but you're talking to me," I told her.

"You talked to me first," she said.

"I wasn't talking to *you*," I said. "I was talking to my sister."

"Fine," she said. And she walked away.

I thought the Great One was right behind

me, with Dad. But when I looked around, I didn't see them. Probably she and Dad were inside the store. So I went in too. It was crowded. I felt like I was swimming through an ocean of legs. Legs and shopping bags and raincoats and dripping umbrellas. I pushed my way through the store, but I couldn't find Dad or the Great One.

I knew the food court and the movies were upstairs. So I got on the Up escalator. I'm not supposed to go on the escalator without holding hands. But I did it anyway. And when I got off, I stood at the top and looked around. No one was watching so I decided to go for it. I decided to do something I've always wanted to try. I walked *down* the Up escalator. And nothing bad happened! Some people looked at me, but nobody said anything. Then I rode it back upstairs.

When I got off the escalator this time, I saw the bookstore. *They must be in there!* I thought. We always stop at the bookstore

when we're at the mall. So I raced through the store until I came to the children's section. I was sure I'd find the Great One sitting in the red beanbag chair with a pile of books. Instead, who was there? The girl from Toy City. *She* was sitting in the beanbag chair, reading. "My sister likes that book," I told her.

She looked up. "You again!" she said. "Are you following me?"

"No," I told her. "Are you following me?"

"How could I be following you when I was here first?"

I didn't answer.

"Where is your sister, anyway? How come she's not with you?"

"I don't need her!" I said. "I know where the food court is and I know where the movie is too."

"You're going to the movies?" she asked. "So am I. What are you going to see?"

"It's a compo . . . it's a compro . . ." I started to say. But I couldn't remember that word.

"Never heard of it," she said. And she went back to her book.

I left the bookstore and looked around. I was angry at Dad for getting lost with the Great One. He should know better. I started to feel funny then. I could feel the thump,

thump, thump of my heart. And a big lump in my throat.

Suddenly, I heard a voice coming from everywhere. At first I thought I was dreaming, because it sounded like Dad. "Jake . . . don't worry, son. We'll find you. You won't be lost for long." It *was* Dad!

"I'm not lost," I said. "You are!"

Dad kept talking. "Don't go anywhere with anyone."

"Okay," I said.

"If you're in a store, tell a salesperson or a cashier who you are. And they'll know what to do," Dad said.

"Okay," I answered again, thinking he could hear me the way I could hear him.

I went into the nearest store. It was the skate and surf store. The music inside was so loud I had to shout at the guy behind the counter. "Hi, I'm Jake."

"Hey, dude," he said to me.

"You know what to do, right?"

"Sorry, dude, I'm really busy right now."

"Should I wait?"

"Up to you, dude."

I decided to go up to the cashier instead.

"I'm Jake," I told him.

"Cool name."

"My dad's looking for me."

"Don't worry, dude. Your secret's safe with me."

What secret? "Maybe I should go to another store," I said.

He shrugged. "Whatever."

When I came out of the dude store, I saw the lights spelling out PIZZA. I ran up to the counter and I said, "I'm Jake."

"What'll you have, Jake?" the server man asked.

"You're supposed to say you found me," I told him.

"Okay, sure." He snapped his fingers like he was a magician. "I found you!"

I told him, "No, not like that."

"What is this?" he asked. "Some kind of knock-knock joke?"

I heard Dad's voice again. "Jake . . . Where are you, Jake?"

"At the pizza place," I said. I'm hungry, so I'm going to eat, okay? You said we could have pizza."

"Yeah, sure kid," the server man said. He thought I was talking to *him*. "What'll it be?"

"I only eat white food," I told him.

"So you want a white pizza?"

"Okay."

"We'll call you when it's ready."

"My name is Jake."

"Yeah, you already said."

Then I heard another voice saying, "Jake is six years old. He's wearing jeans and a gray sweatshirt with a kangaroo on it. He has brown hair and brown eyes. He's missing two front teeth. Please stop a police officer or a security guard if you spot Jake."

I sat down at a table to wait for my food. And suddenly, three big girls surrounded me. They started jumping up and down. "It's him! It's him! You're Jake, right?"

"How do you know my name?" I asked.

"They're only blaring it all over the mall," one of them said.

Then another one shouted, "We found him! We found Jake!" And she waved her arms around.

More people made a circle around me. A woman with curly hair called, "I'll watch him. You get security!"

That's when I got scared. "I want my dad!" I said.

"He wants his dad," they repeated.

"And my sister," I said.

"And his sister," they repeated, like we were doing a play.

"Don't worry, Jake," the woman with the curly hair said. "They'll be here soon."

Then the girl from the bookstore inched in close to the curly-haired woman. She looked at me. "Why didn't you *say* you were lost?"

"I wasn't lost!"

"Do you two know each other?" the curly-haired woman said.

"Not really," the girl said.

"Vera, this is Jake," the curly-haired woman said. "Jake, this is my daughter, Vera."

"I want my dad!" I said again. I thought about crying.

But then Dad was pushing through the crowd. The Great One was right behind him, shoving people out of her way. When Dad spotted me, he called, "Jake!" I jumped up from the table and ran to him. He scooped me up and kissed me a hundred times. He held me so tight I could hardly breathe. But I didn't care.

When he put me down, the Great One said, "Why did you do that?"

"Do what?" I asked.

"Get lost," she said.

"I didn't get lost. You and Dad got lost."

"That's crazy," she argued. "You lost us!"

"No," I said. "I was looking in the window, talking to you. And then you were gone!"

"No, I was walking along talking to Dad, and then *you* were gone!" she said. "And you scared Dad so bad!"

"I did?"

"Yes, but you didn't scare me! I always knew you were okay. I mean, who'd want to steal you? You were just being a pain, same as always!"

"Well, I had a really good time," I told her. "So ha ha! I walked *down* the Up escalator."

"Did you hear that, Dad?" the Great One said. "Did you hear what he did? He walked *down* the Up escalator. And do you know how many times Mom's told him that's dangerous?"

"Abigail," Dad said, taking the Great One's hand. "Jake," he said, taking mine. "Let's just be glad we're all together. Now, how about lunch?"

"Lunch is on the house!" the manager of the pizza place called.

"That's very nice of you," Dad said. "But not necessary."

"I insist," the manager said.

Everyone at the food court cheered.

Then the Great One said, "I'll see that robot movie if you still want to."

And I knew she was glad she found me.

The Great One

"SAY 'CHEESE!'"

We're going to visit Grandpa Pete for his birthday. Fluzzy can't come, so Charlie, our babysitter, is going to watch him. "Goodbye, Fluzzy," I said. But Fluzzy wouldn't look at me. He knew we were going away and leaving him behind. I always feel sad when I have to say goodbye to Fluzzy. I wish I could pack him in my suitcase.

Grandpa Pete lives in Florida. Not the

Disney World part of Florida. Not the beach part, either. He lives in Everglades City. It's the-middle-of-nowhere, Florida. He never comes to visit us because he won't leave his birds. They're not really *his* birds, but that's what he calls them. Every morning and every night Grandpa Pete hangs his binoculars around his neck and goes out in his canoe to watch them. He knows his birds the way Mom and Dad know me and the Pain.

"Maybe we'll see an alligator this time!" the Pain sang. "Maybe we'll see a snake!" The Pain has a book, *Wildlife of the Florida Everglades*. He likes to look at the pictures.

"I don't want to see a snake," I told him.

"One time Justin had a birthday party," the Pain said. "And Reggie Reptile came with his snakes. One of them was a boa constrictor. That was so cool!"

"I don't want to hear any more about snakes!" I shouted.

The Pain laughed.

I decided to wear my cowboy boots on the plane.

"You don't need boots in Florida," Mom said when she saw me.

"Snakes can't bite through leather," I told her.

"Where did you hear that?" she asked.

"I read it in the Pain's book."

Mom shook her head, but she didn't say I couldn't wear my boots.

When we got to Grandpa Pete's, he acted like he saw us yesterday, even though it's been a year. He's not the huggy kind of grandpa. He never says how much we've grown or how glad he is to see us.

"I've got something for you," Grandpa Pete said, holding out two cameras. "Throwaways. You each get twenty-four pictures."

"You mean it's not a digital?" the Pain asked.

"Digital?" Grandpa Pete said, as if he'd never heard the word. "This camera uses

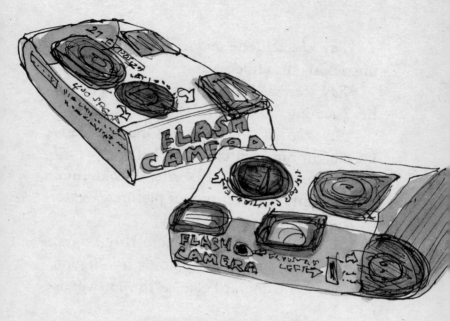

film, Jacob." Grandpa Pete never calls the Pain Jake—only Jacob. "When you've taken all your pictures, the film gets developed into photos. So take your pictures carefully. You can't put more film in this camera."

"Thanks, Grandpa Pete!" I said.

I elbowed the Pain. "Oh, thanks," he said to Grandpa. He was already snapping pictures.

"*Say 'cheese!'*" he said to Dad. He got him unpacking his underwear.

"*Say 'cheese!'*" he said to Mom. He got her yawning.

"*Say 'cheese!'*" he said to Grandpa Pete. He caught him scratching his belly.

"You're going to be sorry," I told him. "You've only got twenty-four pictures."

"So?" he said.

"So, we're going to be here three days. And when you run out, don't ask if you can use my camera, because the answer is *no!*"

"Did I say I want to use your camera?"

"I'm just telling you the rules."

"*Say 'cheese!'*" He snapped a picture of me with my mouth open.

"And stop taking my picture!" I told him. He laughed.

As soon as it was dark, we went to sleep on blow-up mattresses. Grandpa Pete doesn't have a TV. He doesn't have a computer or a cell phone either. His house is just a big screened porch with one small inside room. The screens keep out most of the bugs. There are plenty of bugs. Too many for Mom. She's always swatting at something.

Early the next morning, before the sun came up, Grandpa Pete woke the Pain and me. "Shhhh . . ." he whispered, because Mom and Dad were sound asleep. We got into our long pants, long-sleeve shirts, and floppy hats. We grabbed our cameras. Outside, Grandpa Pete looked down at my cowboy boots.

"You can't wear those in a canoe," he told me.

"But I have to," I said.

"They'll get wet."

"That's okay," I told him. "I don't mind."

"She's afraid of snakes," the Pain told Grandpa Pete. "She thinks they can't bite her if she's wearing boots."

"I always thought it was alligators that couldn't bite through leather," Grandpa Pete said.

Alligators, too? That made me feel even
better about wearing my boots!

Grandpa Pete sprayed us with citronella
to keep away the mosquitoes. Then we
headed for his old Jeep.

Miss Memory was waiting for us. Miss Memory is Grandpa Pete's best friend. No kidding—that's her real name. Memory Clark. She lives next door.

Grandpa Pete said, "I don't have to worry

about forgetting things because I've always got my Memory with me." He makes the same joke every time we visit. The Pain doesn't get it. He says he does, but I can tell he doesn't.

Miss Memory is a birder too. A birder is someone who watches birds. There are more than 350 kinds of birds in the Everglades, and I think Grandpa Pete and Miss Memory know them all.

The Pain got into Grandpa Pete's canoe and I went with Miss Memory. Grandpa Pete has rules for canoeing in the Everglades. Rule number one is look and listen. If we see something interesting, we can point at it, but we can't call out. That's the hardest rule for the Pain. He has no self-control. But he knows Grandpa Pete will leave him behind if he can't keep still. And then he'll never get to see an alligator in the wild.

Canoeing in the Everglades is like being on another planet. It's so quiet. Everywhere you look it's just water, little islands full of birds, and us. No other people. Just the *lap, lap, lap* of our canoes paddling along.

Click. I snapped a picture of a pink and white bird with a beak that looked like a spoon.

Click. I got a shot of a really big turtle.

Click. I got an osprey flying overhead.

Click. I got Grandpa Pete and the Pain in their canoe.

So far, no snakes. And no alligators either. I can't decide if I want to see an alligator or not. Suppose I see one and get so scared I scream? Suppose the alligator swims under our canoe and tips it over? Then what?

We went out in the canoes twice a day, early in the morning and just before sunset. On our last day Miss Memory invited me over to keep her company while she baked a pineapple upside-down cake. "It's your grandpa's favorite," she said.

"My favorite is chocolate," I told her.

"If you come back for your birthday, I'll bake you a chocolate cake."

"That's really nice, but my birthday is July fourth." I didn't want to hurt her feelings. I didn't want to say we have a party every year and all the relatives come, except Grandpa Pete—even though he's invited.

Later, Miss Memory said to Mom and Dad, "I wish you'd stay longer. Three days is nothing."

"I'd say it's just about the right amount of time," Grandpa Pete said. "Any longer and they'd be bored. Or I might get sick of them."

"Pete!" Miss Memory said. "They don't know you're kidding."

"Who's kidding?" Grandpa Pete said.

I couldn't tell if he was or if he wasn't.

"I want to stay until I see an alligator," the Pain said.

"Why don't we just take them to Gatorama on the way to the airport tomorrow?" Mom suggested.

Grandpa Pete gave Mom a look. "That's

for tourists," he said. It's the real deal or nothing for my grandchildren."

Mom grew up in the city. What does she know about alligators?

Just before supper we went out in the canoes again. I must have been hungry, because I was thinking about Miss Memory's pineapple upside-down cake and wondering if I'd like it. I like cake and I like pineapple. But I've never tried them together upside down.

Suddenly, I had a creepy feeling. It wasn't just the quiet or the gray sky. I felt prickles on the back of my neck. I sat up straight, the way Fluzzy does when he knows something is going to happen. And then I saw them. In the distance. First it was just their snouts. Then they lifted their heads. Alligators! I looked over at the Pain. But I could tell he and Grandpa Pete didn't see them yet. If they did, they'd be pointing. I turned my head to look at Miss Memory, but she was paddling along same as always. I was the only one who saw them. Just me. They were my secret! I picked up my camera. *Say "cheese,"* I told them inside my head.

I was already thinking of how I would tell Ms. Valdez, my science teacher, about seeing four alligators. *Right in front of us,* I'd say. *Close enough to touch.* That wasn't true, but it made a better story. I was so glad I was wearing my leather cowboy boots.

But how would I feel if the Pain saw

alligators and didn't tell me? Not that the Pain has ever kept a secret in his entire life. But still, it would be so unfair. So I pointed. Miss Memory stopped paddling and pointed too. Then Grandpa Pete tapped the Pain on his shoulder and pointed. The Pain clapped his hand over his mouth. He was so excited he started rocking the canoe. If he fell in and got eaten by an alligator, Mom and Dad would be really mad at Grandpa Pete.

Two of the alligators crawled up onto one of the small islands. My hands shook as I snapped pictures of them. After a minute Miss Memory started paddling backward, very slowly, very quietly. Grandpa Pete did the same. The alligators didn't see us. At least, I don't think they did.

When we got back to the house, the Pain started yelling, "Alligators! We saw alligators."

"I hope you weren't close to them," Mom said.

"Close enough to touch!" the Pain sang. When he saw the looks on Mom's and Dad's faces he laughed. "Ha ha . . . fooled you, didn't I?"

"So you didn't see alligators?" Dad asked.

"We did!" I told Dad. "Four of them. We took pictures."

"Really, Pete," Mom said to Grandpa. "I hope you were thinking about their safety."

"I always think about the alligators' safety," Grandpa Pete said.

* * *

The next day we flew home. Fluzzy pretended not to care we were back. He had that *I don't even see you!* look on his face. But he couldn't fool me. I knew he'd missed us.

When I got into bed, Mom came in, holding up my boots. "I don't think we're ever going to dry these out." She sniffed inside them and made a face. I already knew they smelled terrible, like the muck we

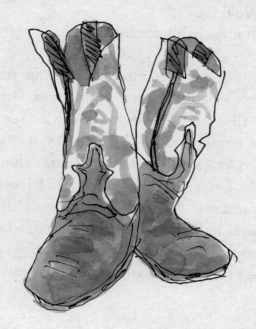

walked through every time we went in the canoes. But I was hoping Mom would know what to do.

"We're going to have to throw them away," she said. "They're ruined."

"But I love those boots!" I cried.

"Well, Abigail . . ." She didn't say anything else. She just carried them out of my room.

"Can I get another pair?" I called.

"We'll see."

That probably meant no.

The next day Dad dropped off our film to be developed. He came home with the pictures that night. I couldn't wait to see how mine turned out. I knew they would be good. I knew they'd be way better than the Pain's. I opened the envelope. I took out the pictures. *What?* I thought as I flipped through half of them. "These can't be my pictures!" I cried. They were so blurry you couldn't make out anything. I grabbed the

Pain's envelope. "Let me see those. . . ."

"Hey!" he said. And before I could stop him he grabbed *my* envelope.

He checked out my pictures while I checked out his. But these couldn't be mine either. They were all black. "You had your finger over the lens," I told the Pain.

"Not every time," he said. "Look at this one!" He held it up. It was a perfect picture of an alligator. "Only our alligators came out right," he said.

But only *my* alligator looked like he was saying "cheese."

FLUZZY IN CHARGE

See if I care if they go away.
See if I care if they leave me home with the
   babysitter.
I'll show them how much I care!

As soon as they're gone I race into *his* room.
His elephant is gone!
He took his elephant with him but not me?

See if I care!

Next, I tear down the hall to *her* room.
I jump onto her bed and sniff everything.
I bite her troll doll.
I pull at its hair.
Then I knock it to the floor and hide it
          under the bed.

When I get thirsty I slurp
from the toilet bowl.

The babysitter says,
Fluzzy, that's disgusting!
You have your own water dish.

See if I care what the babysitter says!

I hide in the mom's closet
      way in back, behind the coats.
The babysitter can't find me.

She calls, *Fluzzy, where are you?*
Fluzzy, what am I going to tell them if you
      get lost?

How can I get lost when she won't let me out
      of the house?

When she finally opens the closet door
      I jump out and hiss at her.

See if I care how loud she screams!

At night I chase toy mice.
I skid across the floor.
Then back again.

She calls, *Fluzzy, you're driving me crazy!*

See if I care!

In the morning I fly down the stairs
        and leap onto the kitchen counter.
I paw at everything.
Spices fall over.
Jelly beans tumble to the floor.
Sugar spills from the bowl.
It crunches when I walk in it, like snow.

Fluzzy! she cries when she sees the mess.
Let's get this straight.
I'm in charge!

Ha ha! That's what *they* think too!

You don't want me to tell them you're a bad
        kitty, do you? she asks.

A bad kitty? Me?
They'd never believe that!

They might not come back if they think you're a
        bad kitty, she says.

But she can't scare me.
They always come back.

And when they do,
I'll pretend I didn't even know they
were gone.

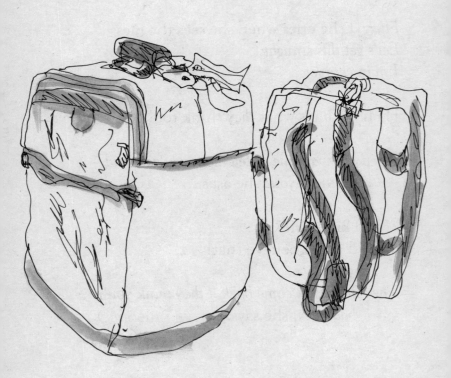

Judy Blume spent her childhood in Elizabeth, New Jersey, making up stories inside her head. She has spent her adult years in many places, doing the same thing, only now she writes her stories down on paper. Her twenty-eight books have won many awards, including the National Book Foundation's Medal for Distinguished Contribution to American Letters.

Judy lives in Key West and New York City. You can visit her at judyblume.com.

James Stevenson has written and illustrated more than a hundred books for children. In forty years at the *New Yorker*, he published more than two thousand cartoons and covers, as well as numerous written pieces. His illustrated column "Lost and Found New York" frequently appears on the op-ed page of the *New York Times*.